WINNER of 27 National & International AWARDS

Stranger in the Woods: The Book

❋ 2004 National Humane Society KIND Award

❋ 2002 Early Childhood News Director's Choice & Judges' Award

❋ 2001 International Reading Association Children's Book Award for Young Readers' Fiction

❋ 2001 American Booksellers Association Book Sense Book of the Year Finalist

❋ 2001 National Christian Schools Children's Crown Gallery Classic Award

❋ 2001 NAPRA Nautilus Award Finalist

❋ 2000 Benjamin Franklin Award for Best Children's Picture Book

Stranger in the Woods: The Soundtrack

❋ 2002 NAPPA Children's Resources Gold Award for Spoken Word & Storytelling

❋ 2002 Film Advisory Board Award of Excellence

Stranger in the Woods: The Movie

❋ 2003 International Wildlife Film Festival Finalist Award

❋ 2002 Wildscreen Panda Awards Finalist

❋ 2002 Aegis Award for Drama/Entertainment

❋ 2002 Communicator Awards for Original Music, Humor & Children's Programming

❋ 2002 Omni Bronze Award

❋ 2002 Telly Award Finalist for Children's Audience & Wildlife Nature

❋ Dove Foundation's Family-Friendly Endorsement

❋ KIDS FIRST! Endorsement

❋ 2002 Film Advisory Board Award of Excellence

❋ 2002 Videographer Awards for Voice-over Talent, Original Music, Humor & Children

A PHOTOGRAPHIC FANTASY

Stranger in the Woods

Carl R. Sams II & Jean Stoick

Acknowledgements:

*W*e would like to thank all the teachers, librarians, moms, dads, grandmas and grandpas
who have shared the magic of *Stranger in the Woods* with children of all ages for ten years.

Thanks to Carol Henson, "The Book Doctor," for editing.
Laura and Rob Sams, and Kim Williams for their suggestions.
Glen Petersen, Tony Beaverson, and Bud Solem of Petersen Productions
for their inspiration and captivating video production.
Dan Goodenow, Karen McDiarmid, Greg Dunn, Mark Hoppstock and
Dave Atkinson of Precision Color for their excellent prepress work.

Special thanks to Brian DePoy our Mac computer specialist,
for countless hours keeping our computers up and running.
His son Brandon, who was wonderfully patient in building snowmen.
Sue Boyd, our publicist, and Danny Boyd for their video skills and
for sharing their ideas on this book. Their daughter Nancy,
our expert on placing carrot noses on snowmen.

Carl R. Sams II Photography, Inc.

361 Whispering Pines
Milford, MI 48380
800/552-1867 248/685-2422 Fax 248/685-1643
www.strangerinthewoods.com   www.carlsams.com

Title Design: Douglas Alden Peterson
Visualeyes of Brighton, Michigan

Publisher's Cataloging-In-Publication Data
Sams, Carl R.
Stranger in the Woods: a photographic fantasy
by Carl R. Sams II & Jean Stoick — Milford, MI
Carl R. Sams II Photography, Inc. © 2010
p.cm.
Summary: The resident birds and animals react to a
snowman appearing in their woods after a winter storm.

Printed and bound: Friesens of Altona, Manitoba, Canada.
September 2010 – 55827

Lenticular printing: World 3D, USA
August 2010 – 080310

ISBN 978-0-9827625-0-9
1. Snowman–Juvenile fiction.
2. [Snowman–Fiction] I. Stoick, Jean. II. Title.

Library of Congress Control Number: 2010911540

10 9 8 7 6 5 4 3 2 1

*For those who protect wild places
and to the snowman that lives
in every child's heart.*

The snowflakes were
resting after their twisting
twirling dance through
the crisp night air.

Every twig in the forest
wore a new coat
of glimmering white.

Daybreak came
softly moving through the woods
and yawning
as its rays slowly stretched
across the snowy meadows.

The birds
were the first to notice...

Stranger in the woods!

"Take care!
  Take care!"
The bluejays cawed
  a warning
    from high in the tops
      of the tall oaks.

Stranger in the woods!

"Do you hear the jays calling?"
Mother Doe spoke softly
to her fawn.

"Yes," he whispered.
"I always listen to the birds,
the wind blowing through the trees,
the rustling of the leaves
and all the sounds of the woods."

Stranger in the woods!

"Who-hoo's in the woods?
Where? Where did the jays say?
Where is he?"
asked the Owl of Many Questions.

"Coo-coo-could that be him?"
asked the mourning dove.
"There!
Beyond the old apple tree.
Follow the snow trail, past the pond
to where the meadow begins.
Not far... not far at all."

"Who-hoo's in the woods?
Why is he here?
When? When did the stranger come?"
asked the Owl of Many Questions.

"I've been here since early morning,
before the first pale light
on the Eastern Sky,"
said the munching muskrat.
"No stranger came this way.
No one passed by my pond."

"I followed the snow trail
under the light of the Winter Moon,"
answered the buck.

"He was not there during the night,
that I am sure!"

As the animals moved
through the snowy forest, they came to
the edge of the meadow.

The frightened doe
stomped her hoof
and snorted!

"Where is he?
Where is he?
Can you see him?"

"Yes! Yes! I do see him!"
        chattered the squirrel.

"Someone needs to go and,
        and check-check-check
                check'em out!"

"Who-hoo-hoo will go?
Who-hoo-hoo will go see?"
asked the Owl of Many Questions.

"Now don't be looking at me.
I'm much too busy chew-chew-chewing on my antler,"
sputtered the porcupine.

"You'll not be volunteering me!
No sir-ree!"
said the scared rabbit.

"Is... is he watching me?"

"Howdy-dee-dee.
It is me, the chickadee-dee-dee!
I will go! I will take the lead."

"I'm-m-m-m the smallest and
I ca-ca-can scamper quickly.
I'll do it! I'll make a tunnel under the snow
where only I can go...

...creeping in closer to get a look.
Quietly
just like a m-m-mouse!"

"Let it be me!
    Let me go!"
volunteered the fawn.

"I can do it.
    I know I can!"

"I am the strongest and the biggest," said the young buck.

"I should go first."

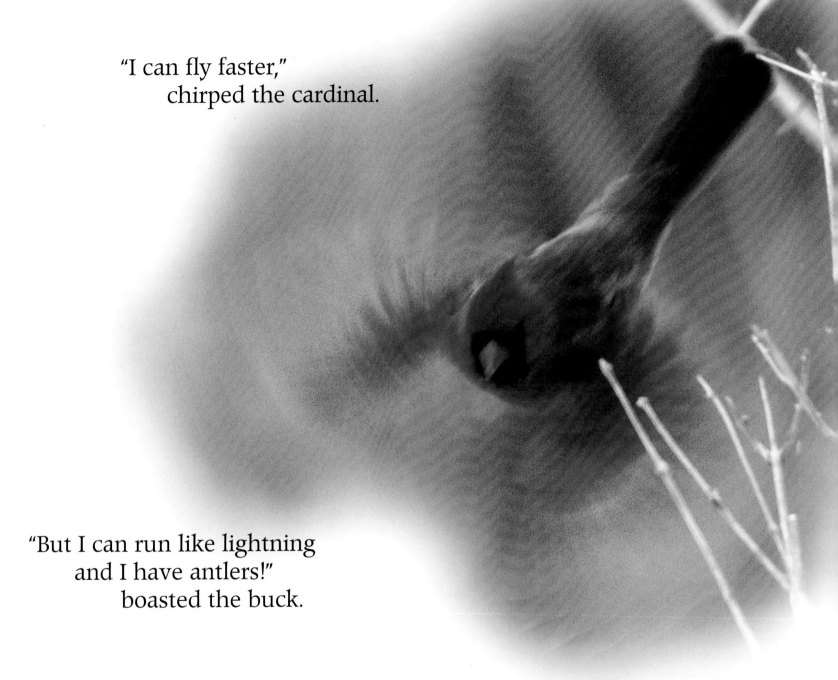

"I can fly faster,"
   chirped the cardinal.

"But I can run like lightning
   and I have antlers!"
      boasted the buck.

"But... I am... I am... RED!"
   announced the cardinal,
      not knowing what else to say.

"What are you waiting for? I'm there already-dee-dee!" exclaimed

the Chickadee-dee-dee!

"Gee-gee-gee!"
said the Chickadee-dee-dee.
"There are nuts and seeds
on his hat for you and me!

This stranger is friendly.
Come see! Come see!
There's plenty."

"I can see there's something for you,"
said the buck. "Could it be there's something for me?
My nose is leading me to corn
buried beneath the snow."

"I found a treat that I can eat,"
said the young doe as she reached out
to the stranger.

"Wow! A carrot!
Do I have to share it?"

"What is this?" questioned the fawn
as he passed a curious object in the snow.

"Could it be...
there's more than one stranger in the woods?"

After the corn was gone,
the animals left by the snow trail one by one
and disappeared into the winter woods.

It was the chickadee who took the last seed and flew away.

The snowman stood alone...
but only for a short time.

"They have eaten everything...
even the carrot nose,"
whispered the little sister
peeking out from behind the evergreens.

"Let's put out more
              seeds and corn
before they come back,"
        encouraged the brother.

"The animals will never know
        we were here."

"How long will
we feed them?"
she asked.

"For a long,
long time,"
he replied.

"After the snow has gone
and the snowman has melted away,
until the frogs start to sing
and the trees grow new leaves."

I think they like carrots the best!

THE END

Recipe for a Snowman

Ingredients:

    1 Generous Helping of
       Wet Packing Snow

  ¼ Cup of Round Nuts in the Shell

    2 Larger Nuts

    1 Large Carrot

    2 Old Gloves or Mittens

    1 Old Hat

    2 Fallen Branches

1-4 Well-Bundled Children

    2 Scoops of Imagination

    1 Dash of Good Humor

May substitute or add any
of the following ingredients:

    Scarf
    Ear muffs
    Sunglasses
    Acorns
    Pine Cones

Makes one serving.
May last for several days.

Preheat a winter's day
to 32° F or 0° C.

Firmly pack a ball of snow between your two hands and place upon the ground. Continue to roll on snow covered ground until the ball gathers enough snow to measure about three feet. This will form the base of your snowman.

Roll and shape two additional snowballs. The first will be approximately one foot in diameter and the second will be two feet. Place the second largest ball on top of the base. The smallest is the head and goes on top.

Press in the smaller nuts to form the teeth. To give the snowman a smile, nuts should be placed higher on the outer corners of mouth. Center a carrot above the mouth for the nose. Push in the larger end with pointed end out (refer to snowman picture). The two largest nuts form the eyes and are to be placed above the carrot nose.

Attach fallen branches to the middle ball of snow on either side for the arms. Add gloves or mittens on the ends of the sticks. Top him off with an old hat and sprinkle with laughter. Toss in a brief snowball fight for excitement. Garnish with seeds on top of hat and scatter corn around snowman for additional enjoyment.